Elf and the City

Adapted by Leslie Goldman

Based on the screenplay by David Berenbaum

PRICE STERN SLOAN

Cover photo: Peter Tangen / © 2003 New Line Productions

Published by Price Stern Sloan, a division of Penguin Young Readers Group,
345 Hudson Street, New York, NY 10014.
PSS! is a registered trademark of Penguin Group (USA) Inc.

Printed in the United States of America. Published simultaneously in Canada.

ISBN 0-8431-0772-3   A B C D E F G H I J

❄ Chapter One ❄

Buddy the Elf had been living in the North Pole for as long as he could remember. He was raised as an elf, and he grew up believing he was an elf. Then one day he got some surprising news: It turns out he wasn't an elf at all—he was a regular person from New York City! Suddenly Buddy understood why he was always freezing and hitting his head in doorways. It was time for him to go home to meet his real dad.

The trip to New York City was not easy. Buddy had to walk through a dark cave filled with large and scary beasts. They had bright, shiny eyes and, rather than walking on two or four legs, these beasts traveled on rolling wheels. Most had only four, but some had many more!

Buddy later learned that these beasts were actually cars and trucks, and the cave

was the Lincoln Tunnel. But this didn't make the experience any less strange.

Swallowing his fear, Buddy inched through the tunnel as the hulking beasts whizzed by. Once he made it to the other side, he was amazed. New York City looked just like it did in his snow globe!

It was nothing like the North Pole, which had lots of snow and trees, and a bunch of elves. In New York there were tall buildings everywhere, and tons of people. They all walked very fast. And when Buddy said hello, no one answered him.

"Hi," he said. "Happy afternoon!

Salutations!" Buddy tried talking louder. "HELLO!" he shouted.

Finally a woman waved to him. Excited, Buddy waved back. He went over to introduce himself, but before he got there, the woman got into a yellow beast and they sped away.

Buddy kept walking. Soon he saw something magical! It was sort of like a merry-go-round, but there was nowhere to sit! Buddy walked through the revolving door, but he didn't get out. It was too much fun. He spun around and around, yelling, "Wheeeeeeeee!"

Soon someone asked him to leave, which was okay with Buddy. By now he was dizzy, and he also figured someone else might want a turn on the ride.

New York City was filled with wondrous things. Buddy could hardly believe his eyes when he saw a sign that read, WORLD'S BEST CUP OF COFFEE!

He ran into the diner and shouted, "Congratulations to you all! You did it! That's wonderful."

Everyone stared at Buddy. Guessing that they were over the thrill, he continued on his way.

Seconds later he noticed something on the ground. Free chewing gum! Buddy was excited. Scraping it off the ground, he popped it into his mouth. He chewed it with a smile. But then he realized it tasted like dirt!

After he spit out his gum, Buddy decided it was time to find his dad. He was in New York for a reason, after all.

He pulled out his snow globe and compared the picture to the giant building in front of

Michael Gingsburg / © 2003 New Line Productions.

him. It was the Empire State Building, where his dad worked!

Buddy got onto the elevator. It was filled with people wearing suits and serious expressions. Some of them looked at Buddy's strange elf outfit, and others just looked away. But Buddy was too happy to notice. He started to whistle.

"Can you press sixty-seven, please?" asked a man in a suit.

Buddy looked at all of the numbered circles, and gently pushed the one with the number 67 on it. When it lit up, he gasped. "Hey, that's pretty!" Then he pressed all seventy-five buttons. He pointed cheerfully at all the bright and shiny circles and said, "Look at that!"

As the elevator stopped at every single floor, the other people riding it got angrier and angrier. But Buddy was thrilled.

Reaching his dad's floor, Buddy stepped off the elevator. The first person he saw was a dark-haired woman sitting behind a desk.

"Buddy the Elf is here to see Mr. Walter Hobbs, please."

Walter Hobbs's secretary, Deb, blinked back at Buddy. Assuming he was playing some sort of joke, she said, "You look hilarious. Who sent you?"

"Papa Elf, from the North Pole," Buddy explained with a straight face.

Deb let out a laugh. "Papa Elf? That's rich." Deb sent Buddy right into Walter's office because she thought he was a singing Christmas telegram.

"Dad?" said Buddy. He looked at Walter hopefully, and readjusted his hat and vest.

"Oh, um, all right." Walter crossed his arms over his chest and leaned back in his chair. "Let's get this over with," he said in a tired voice.

Buddy stared at the man who was his father, wondering where to begin. "I walked all day and night to find you."

Walter played along. "Looks like you came from the North Pole."

Buddy's eyes widened happily. "That's exactly where I came from. Santa must have called you!"

"Yeah, I just got off my cell with him," said Walter.

Now Buddy was confused. "Got off what?"

Glancing at his watch impatiently, Walter asked, "Are you going to sing a song or something, or can I get back to work?"

"A song? Anything for you, Dad! Let's see..." Buddy paused as he tried to think of something appropriate. "*I'm here with my dad,*" he sang, completely out of tune. "*I've never met him before, and he wants me to sing a song. I was adopted, and you didn't know I was born. But I'm here and I love you, Dad.*" Buddy rushed forward and gave Walter a hug.

Walter was too surprised to know what to do. "Wow, that was weird. Usually you guys just put my name into 'Jingle Bells' or something."

Realizing that his dad was confused, Buddy shouted, "It's me, your son! Susan

Welles had me and didn't tell you, but now I'm here. It's me—Buddy!"

Walter gasped. For the first time, he knew that the giant elf might not be joking, and if he was, well, then, it just wasn't funny. "Susan Welles? Did you just say Susan Welles? Who sent this Christmas-Gram?" he demanded.

Once more, Buddy was confused. "What's a Christmas-Gram?" he asked, thinking New York City sure was a strange place.

Deb had come into Walter's office, and Walter leaned toward her, whispering, "We may want to call security."

"I already did," Deb whispered back.

Buddy leaned in and said, "I like to whisper, too."

❦ Chapter Two ❧

Five minutes later, two security guards escorted Buddy out of the building. "My dad runs this whole company!" he told them proudly. "I'll bet he's a genius."

"Must run in the family," one of the security guards answered sarcastically.

"You guys are strong!" said Buddy.

Michael Gingsburg / © 2003 New Line Productions.

"Now be a good little elf and go back to Santa Land," said the other guard.

The first guard laughed. "Yeah, go back to Gimbel's."

"Bye, Glenn! Bye, Chris!" Buddy called as he waved to his new friends.

Looking across the street, Buddy saw something magical. It was Gimbel's department store, and it was all decked out for Christmas.

Buddy was so excited, he didn't think to look both ways before crossing the street.

Crash! Bang! A car hit Buddy, and he went flying.

Standing up, he skipped back toward the store, shouting and waving, "I'm okay! Thank you! Thanks, everyone!" The speeding beast hadn't even stopped, and Buddy was happy that it wasn't harmed.

Buddy walked into the store and suddenly found himself in the middle of a fabulous winter wonderland. Candy canes lined the aisle. Colored lights sparkled. Tinsel winked.

Giant trees covered with bright and shiny ornaments towered overhead. For a minute, Buddy felt like he was back at the North Pole.

As he stood there gaping, a perfume lady approached. "Passion fruit spray?" she asked.

Buddy's eyes bulged. "Fruit spray! For real?" He couldn't believe his luck. First he finds the best coffee in the world, and then he chews free gum, and now, fruit in a spray! Opening his mouth, he closed his eyes.

The clerk stared at him for a few seconds.

"Ready when you are," Buddy insisted. He couldn't wait to taste the sweet and delicious fruit blend on his tongue.

The clerk looked around, wondering if this was some sort of joke. But when the man in the elf suit didn't move, she decided to spray.

"Blech!" yelled Buddy as he stumbled backward, horrified. He wiped off his tongue with his hands, but the nasty taste lingered. His tongue was swelling up, and he felt like he was going to be sick. The fruit spray tasted even worse than the free gum!

When the horrible flavor finally faded, Buddy explored the rest of Gimbel's. Turning the corner, he could hardly believe his eyes. Moving stairs! Buddy had never seen such an amazing thing.

He stopped at the edge of the escalator and looked up, transfixed. Customers got on and off, making it look so easy. But Buddy was nervous. He approached the moving staircase and stood before it, puzzled. Tons of people started lining up behind him, wondering what the holdup was.

"Are you going or what?" asked an impatient shopper.

"Um, yeah," Buddy said warily.

He stepped forward with one leg, but kept the other planted firmly on the ground. The stairs kept moving, forcing his legs to split. "Jiminy Christmas!" he yelled.

Once he recovered, Buddy decided to take the elevator instead. But when he got on, he stood backward, face-to-face with another shopper. Buddy stared at him, which just made the shopper angry. "You think you're pretty smart, huh?" asked the man.

"I'm not that smart," said Buddy, smiling bashfully. "But thanks."

He got off the elevator seconds before the angry man was about to explode.

Soon after, another man in an elf suit walked up to Buddy and yelled, "What are you doing up here? Get to the ninth floor right away!"

"Okay," said Buddy, who didn't have anything better to do, anyway.

A few minutes later, Buddy was in Gimbel's version of Santa Land on the ninth floor. But he wasn't very happy about it.

"This snow looks fake," he said to the first person he saw, who happened to be the store manager.

"It's white, ain't it?" asked the manager, shooting Buddy an impatient glare, and wondering who this guy thought he was.

"Snow doesn't just pile up unless it's moving through the use of a tool, such as a shovel," Buddy explained. "I would give this some natural erosion—a slight wind-drift look."

The cranky manager looked at Buddy like he was crazy—a look that Buddy was getting used to. "What the heck are you talking about? Erosion? Don't touch the snow! And what are you smiling about? You think this is a joke?"

"Oh no," said Buddy. "I'm just smiling. Smiling is my favorite."

"Well, take it down a notch."

Buddy tried to frown, but his lips started to quiver and ache. It hurt too much! He smiled again, in the exact same way.

"All right, smiley," said the manager. "Sweep the tinfoil off this path. Santa's going to be here at nine A.M., sharp!"

"Santa?" Buddy was so excited. He could barely contain himself. Sure, New York was an interesting place, but he was a little homesick. Jumping up and down victoriously, he yelled, "Oh…My…Gosh…" He turned back to the man and asked, "Wait—you mean Santa Claus, right?"

"Yeah," said the manager. "Where have you been?"

"The North Pole," Buddy told him.

"Ha, ha!" The manager broke out into a smile that lasted for less than a second. "Start elfing. And don't touch the snow!"

Buddy looked around and noticed a new,

very pretty elf. Jovie was hanging ornaments on a Christmas tree.

"Enjoying the view?" she asked him sarcastically.

"Yes, I am." Buddy moved toward her. "I was just standing over there and I thought you looked pretty, so I came over here to tell you that you look pretty."

Jovie gazed at Buddy and tried to figure out if he was crazy or joking. "Why are you messing with me like this? Did someone put you up to it?"

"I'm not messing with you," said Buddy. "It's nice to meet a human who loves elf culture as much as I do."

Jovie laughed. "I wouldn't say I love it. I'm just trying to get through the holidays."

Buddy's mouth dropped open in shock. "Get through? Christmas is the greatest day in the whole wide world!"

"Well, someone's been drinking too much punch. Believe me, after a few years of this, you'll learn to tune it all out."

"Uh-oh," said Buddy. "It sounds like some-one needs to sing a Christmas carol."

Jovie just shook her head. She was so surprised a minute later when Buddy started to sing.

"*The best way to spread Christmas cheer is singing loud for all to hear!*" he belted out.

She took a few steps back. "Well, thanks, but I don't sing."

"Oh, it's easy," said Buddy. "It's just like talking, only louder and longer!"

"Well, I can sing," said Jovie. "I just *don't* sing, especially in front of other people. I could never do that."

"Never? If you can sing by yourself, you can sing anywhere," said Buddy. "There's no difference."

"Actually there's a big difference," said Jovie.

"No, there isn't. Watch!" said Buddy. "*I'm in a store and I'm singing. People are here, and I'm in a store!*" His voice got louder and louder with each word.

Shoppers stared at Buddy as if he was crazy, and Jovie was beginning to wonder the same thing.

"*The store is all shiny, and I'm in a store!*" yelled Buddy. "See?"

"Wow." Jovie took a few more steps away from Buddy.

A loud voice came over the loudspeaker and interrupted Buddy. "Attention, shoppers," it said. "Gimbel's will be closing in ten minutes. Please make your final purchases."

Jovie and the other elves looked relieved.

"Dismissed," said Jovie as she started to leave.

"You're going?" asked Buddy, amazed. "But Santa is coming."

Assuming he was joking, Jovie started to laugh. "Yeah, I'll see you tomorrow. Um, what's your name?"

"Buddy."

"I'm Jovie."

A few minutes later, the lights flickered off, and the doors closed and locked.

When the security guard patrolled the ninth floor, Buddy was careful to hide from him among a stack of toys. Noticing a cute fire truck, Buddy picked it up and read the label on the bottom. "They have elves in Taiwan?" he wondered to himself, amazed.

Chapter Three

Since Buddy had all night alone in the empty department store, he decided to do a little redecorating. After touching up Santa Land, he wrote a sign in sparkly paint that read, WELCOME SANTA! LOVE, BUDDY.

The very next morning, the shoppers at Gimbel's were amazed. Everyone loved the new and improved Santa Land.

Jovie and Buddy were talking when the manager marched up to them. "This is Santa Land," he scolded. "Not stand-around-and-talk-to-each-other-land. Get busy. Santa's here."

"Santa?" yelled Buddy, looking around. "Santa is here?" Noticing a man in a familiar red suit, Buddy rushed forward. "Santa, it's me! Buddy!" He was overjoyed. Sure, New York was fun, but Buddy missed his old friends from the North Pole.

When he finally reached the man in the red suit, he tapped him on the shoulder. The man turned around, and Buddy gasped. "Who the heck are you?"

"Why, I'm Santa Claus," said the man.

"No, you're not!" said Buddy, stamping one foot on the ground.

"Well, of course I am. Ho, ho, ho!"

Buddy crossed his arms over his chest and narrowed his eyes at the imposter. "If you're Santa, then tell me, what song did I sing for you on your birthday last year?"

"Why, you sang 'Happy Birthday,'" said the man in the Santa suit.

"He's right," Buddy said to the group of kids who had gathered around.

Sitting down in his chair, Santa said, "Why don't you cool it, buddy?"

"But you're lying," said Buddy. "I know it." He grabbed Santa's beard and pulled down. It came right off. Buddy stared at the thing in his hands, completely horrified. "AAAHH!" he yelled. "His beard is fake. Impostor! He's an impostor! Get him, kids."

Buddy attacked Santa, and all the kids joined in, wrestling the man to the ground. The manager dove in, trying to help. Then came the parents, and then some elves. It was a huge mess.

Jovie looked on, giggling.

Later that day, though, things didn't seem

so funny. Buddy had landed in jail. He sat on a narrow, smelly cot and looked around. Everything was gray and dreary. There was no sign of Christmas anywhere. Buddy had never been to such a horrible place.

Burying his head in his pillow, he started to cry.

The prisoner Buddy shared his cell with was disgusted at first. But seeing the man dressed in the elf suit crying made him so sad, he started to cry, too.

Later that day, Walter came to the prison to bail Buddy out.

"Dad!" Buddy stepped out of his jail cell and gave Walter a huge hug. "I knew you'd come! I love that you came and I love you, Dad! Know how much I love you?" Buddy spread his arms out. "This much! Except my arms would have to be way longer, like pterodactyl wings."

"All right, pal." Walter pulled away from Buddy and asked, "Who the heck are you, and what's your problem?"

"I'm Buddy, your son," Buddy said again,

confused because he thought he'd already made that point.

"Is this some sort of game?" asked Walter. "Do you want some money?"

"I just want to meet you, and I thought that maybe you might want to meet me, too. I thought we could make gingerbread houses and eat cookie dough and go ice-skating and hold hands."

Walter didn't know what was going on. All he knew was that he couldn't let this giant man in an elf suit wander around alone in New York City. He might get hurt! Or end up in jail again.

Walter took Buddy back to his home and told him to stay there. Then Walter returned to his office. He wondered what his wife and his other son, Michael, would think when they came home to meet a man in an elf suit.

Chapter Four

*A*lone in Walter's apartment, Buddy got bored. The place was a little dull, so he decided to surprise everyone by creating a winter wonderland scene. It was almost Christmas, after all.

By the time Buddy finished he was very hungry, so he went to the kitchen and ate some frosting—straight from the container!

"Buddy?" said Walter, when he came home later that day. "This is my wife, Emily."

"Emuree!" Buddy said with his mouth full. Jumping up, he gave her a hug. "Dad hasn't told me anything about you," he continued, wiping some frosting off his chin.

Just then, Walter and Emily's son, Michael, came home. "Why is Mom hugging Robin Hood?" he asked.

At dinner that night, Buddy told Walter, Emily, and Michael how he had come to New

York. "Then I traveled through seven levels of the candy cane forest, and past the sea of swirly, twirly gumdrops. And then I walked through the Lincoln Tunnel. Can you pass the soda, pretty please?"

When Michael handed Buddy the bottle, he chugged the entire thing.

"So where exactly have you been for the last thirty years?" asked Emily.

"The North Pole!" said Walter. "He's an elf. That's where elves live."

"He's right," said Buddy. "Can you pass the maple syrup, pretty please?"

Alan Markfield / © 2003 New Line Productions.

"I'm sorry but I didn't set out any syrup," said Emily. "It's spaghetti."

"It's okay. I'll get it," said Buddy.

"You like sugar, huh?" asked Emily.

"Is there sugar in syrup?" asked Buddy as he poured the entire bottle onto his dinner.

"Yes," said Emily.

"Then yes," said Buddy. "We elves try to stick to the four basic food groups: candy, candy canes, candy corns, and syrup."

"So will you be staying with us, then?" Emily asked.

Buddy's eyes widened. "You mean I can stay?"

"Emily!" Walter barked.

"Oh, don't be silly." Emily gave her husband a dirty look and then smiled at Buddy. "Of course you can. How long do you think you'll be with us?"

Buddy scratched his head as he thought. "Well, I hadn't really planned it out," he said. "But I was thinking like, forever."

Walter started choking on his spaghetti. When he recovered, he said, "Emily, can I please speak to you in the kitchen?"

When they left, Michael stared at Buddy but didn't say anything.

Looking around the room, Buddy started to feel something rise up out of his stomach. Then he let out a huge belch! "Did you hear that?" he asked Michael.

Wide-eyed and speechless, Michael just nodded.

Later that night, Buddy asked Walter to tuck him in.

"What?" said Walter.

Buddy rearranged the sheets and said, "I can't fall asleep if I'm not tucked in."

"I'm not tucking you in," Walter growled.

"I promise I'll go right to sleep," said Buddy.

"Fine." Walter marched over and tucked Buddy in.

"Tickle fight," said Buddy, poking Walter in the ribs.

"No, Buddy. Stop!" Walter backed away.

"Sorry," said Buddy.

"Just lie down and go to sleep, okay?"

"Do you want to hear a story?" asked Buddy.

Softening his voice, Walter spoke to Buddy as if he were a child. "No, I don't want to hear a story. When this light goes off, you are not getting up, understand?"

"Understand." Buddy fluffed his pillow.

When Walter flicked off the lights, Buddy said, "Dad?"

"Yes, Buddy."

"I love you."

"Go to sleep," said Walter.

"Do you love me?" asked Buddy.

"Yeah, sure." Walter flicked the lights back on and stared at the giant man in an elf costume who claimed to be his son. "Now go to sleep."

"How much do you love me?" asked Buddy. "Like on a scale of one to ten?"

"Well," said Walter, "I haven't known you for very long, but I would say my feelings are . . . significant."

"Significant," Buddy repeated with a happy, sleepy sigh.

"Good night," said Walter. He turned off the lights and closed the door.

Buddy was left all alone in the dark. "Dad?" he said. When there was no response, he raised his voice. "Dad?"

Still not hearing any reply, he said, "Dad?" again. "Dad?" he yelled, starting to panic. "Dad!" Each time he said the word, his voice got louder, until finally he shouted, "Dad!" at the top of his lungs.

Finally, Walter swung the door open. "What?"

"Hi!" said Buddy.

Walter slammed the door closed, and once again, Buddy said, "Dad?"

 Chapter Five

"This sure is something," said Emily, staring into the kitchen the next morning. Buddy had prepared a huge breakfast of spaghetti, and had set the table elaborately.

"Want some more?" asked Buddy.

"Sure, why not?" Emily held out her plate. "So how'd you sleep last night?"

"Great," said Buddy. "I got a full forty minutes and still had time to build a rocking horse."

When Emily noticed the beautiful rocking horse, she almost choked on her spaghetti. "Where did you get the wood?" she asked.

"Why is the TV on the floor?" Walter asked as he walked into the room.

Emily went into the living room and saw that Buddy had dismantled the entertainment center. Sawdust and paint

littered the living room floor. Coming back into the kitchen, she said, "Good morning, honey. Buddy made us breakfast. Isn't that nice?"

Looking at the piles of spaghetti, Walter didn't know what to say.

"He packed us lunches, too."

Buddy pointed to three brown paper bags, all filled with more spaghetti. They were labeled EMILY, WALTER, and MICHAEL in beautiful calligraphy.

"Well, I've got to run. Thanks for breakfast, Buddy," said Emily as she grabbed a bag. "And for lunch!"

"Bye, Emily!" said Buddy.

Buddy plunged the serving spoon into the pot and lifted up a huge mass of spaghetti. "How many scoops?" he asked Walter.

"I'm going to stick with coffee for now," said Walter. "But listen, Buddy, I wanted to talk to you."

"Good," said Buddy. "I wanted to talk to you, too. I've planned out our whole day." He held up a list written in calligraphy. "First, we make snow angels for two hours, then we go ice-skating, and then we eat a tube of cookie dough as fast as we can, and then, to wrap up the day, we snuggle!"

Walter held up his hands. "Buddy, I have to go to work. And another thing: If you're going to be staying around here, you should think about getting rid of this costume. We've got neighbors, you know?"

Buddy looked down at himself, entirely confused. "But I've worn this my whole life."

"Yeah, well, you're not in the North Pole anymore."

Buddy stared at Walter. He knew that New York couldn't be any more different from the North Pole, but he wasn't sure what his dad was suggesting.

"You said you wanted to make me happy, didn't you?" asked Walter.

Buddy nodded his head vigorously. "More than anything."

"Then lose the tights," said Walter.

A few minutes later, Walter left for work. It wasn't long before his phone rang. "Hello?" said Walter.

"It worked!" yelled Buddy, jumping up and down. "It's you."

Walter scowled as he asked, "How did you get this number?"

"Emily left an emergency list."

"Is there an emergency?" asked Walter.

"There's a horrible sound coming from the evil box by the window. It sounds like this . . ." Buddy started to wheeze and hiss and moan.

"That's not evil," said Walter. "It's the radiator. The heat makes noise when it comes on."

"No, it's not," said Buddy as he investigated the strange machine. "Wait, yes it is. You were right! Everything is fine."

"I'm hanging up now," said Walter.

"Okay, I love you," said Buddy. "I'll call you in five minutes! I love you!"

"You don't need to call me, okay?"

"Good idea," said Buddy. "You call me!"

"Okay, I'm hanging up now," said Walter.

"I tuned the piano."

"I'm hanging up…"

"I love you," said Buddy.

Chapter Six

Emily told Buddy that his new brother, Michael, would be home around three, but it was only two, and Buddy was lonely. He decided to meet Michael at school instead.

Once he found the right building, he sat outside, watching as dozens of kids streamed out the front doors.

Spotting his brother, he waved his arms around in the air and jumped up and down. "Michael, Michael!" he yelled.

"Oh man," said Michael, turning away because he was so embarrassed.

"It's me. Your brother. Hey, Michael!"

As kids noticed Buddy, they started to laugh. Michael stormed off. He went into the park, but Buddy followed, shouting, "Michael, wait up!"

"Why is your coat so big?" asked Buddy.

"It's a style," Michael grumbled, totally embarrassed about being seen with a man wearing an elf suit.

"So how was school?" asked Buddy, starting to skip. "Was school fun? Did you get a lot of homework? Do you have a best friend? Does he have a big coat, too? Wanna build a fort?"

Michael spun around to face Buddy. Getting up in his face, he shouted, "Leave!"

Just then a snowball plowed into the back of Buddy's head. "Ow! Peanut brittle! Son of a nutcracker!" He rubbed the spot on his head where the snowball had landed.

Michael couldn't help but laugh, until he got hit in the shoulder.

Seconds later a whole slew of snowballs rained down on the two of them. They were coming from a crowd of older kids.

"Oh no!" Michael's whole face clouded over. "These guys are bad news. We'd better get out of here."

Buddy looked at the crowd. "We can take them. Make as many snowballs as you can."

"There are too many of them," said Michael as he quickly packed together a couple of snowballs. Turning around to Buddy, he noticed that Buddy had already rounded up about thirty.

Buddy asked, "Are you ready?"

"Yeah," said Michael with a slight grin.

Buddy and Michael flung the balls at the older kids. Buddy threw his so hard, they

traveled too quickly to be seen. One by one they nailed the bullies in the face. As soon as a kid raised a snowball, it exploded out of his hand.

Michael watched in awe as Buddy scanned the field for foes, taking kids out one by one. Then he got back to work, lobbing snowballs at a much slower pace.

Suddenly Buddy yelled, "NO!"

A snowball headed straight for Michael, but Buddy managed to throw one in a counterattack. Buddy's snowball hit the one headed for Michael and knocked it off course. They both exploded and then fell to the ground just in time, missing Michael by a few inches.

Seeing this masterful move, the remaining bully took off, fleeing down the path toward the playground a hundred yards away. Buddy carefully packed a new snowball and aimed it at the kid. Letting it sail, the snowball hit him in the back of the head, hard enough to knock the bully off balance and send him headfirst into the snow.

Michael just looked at Buddy with awe. "Where did you say you were from?" he asked.

Chapter Seven

*A*fter showing Michael the new Christmas display at Gimbel's, Buddy took him to the ninth floor. He was looking for a certain pretty elf.

"You like her?" Michael asked, noticing Buddy staring at Jovie.

"Like who?" asked Buddy.

"That girl you're staring at."

"Um, yes," said Buddy.

"Why don't you ask her out?" asked Michael.

Buddy asked, "Out to where?"

As Jovie noticed them, she started to come closer.

Buddy grabbed on to Michael's elbow. "We should leave," he said. "I need to leave, fast."

"Don't leave," said Michael. "Ask her out."

"Out?" asked Buddy.

"On a date, you know. To eat food."

"Food?" Buddy quivered as Jovie approached.

"If she says yes, you're in. It's like a secret code that girls have," Michael explained.

Before Buddy could ask Michael what he was talking about, Jovie was right there. "Well, look who it is," she said.

"Jovie! This is my bro—" Buddy didn't finish his sentence because Michael wasn't there anymore.

"I was wondering if I'd ever see you again. So did Gimbel's give you your job back?"

"No, but it worked out pretty good." Buddy smiled. "They gave me a restraining order."

Jovie glanced around nervously. "Then you should really get out of here."

"But I really wanted to see you," said Buddy. "You're beautiful, and I feel warm when I'm around you."

"You're the weirdest guy I've ever met in my life," said Jovie.

"Weird like good?" asked Buddy hopefully.

Jovie couldn't help but grin. "I haven't decided."

"So, do you want to eat food?"

Jovie looked at him like he was crazy, but as usual, Buddy didn't even notice. "Do you want to eat food?"

"Do I want to eat food?" Jovie repeated, perplexed.

"You know." Buddy winked and lowered his voice. "The code."

"I just took my lunch break," said Jovie. "But I'm free on Thursday night."

Buddy smiled slowly, and then he started to dance around. "Yes!" he yelled, pumping his arm in the air.

That night, Walter came home to a surprising sight.

Buddy and Michael were decorating a giant Christmas tree.

"Where did that come from?" asked Walter.

"Buddy chopped it down in the park!" said Michael.

Walter went to talk to Emily in another room while Michael unwound a spool of Christmas lights.

"How are we going to put the star on top?" asked Michael.

"I've got it," said Buddy. He catapulted himself off the couch and into the tree. Unfortunately, he overshot his target and landed smack against the wall.

"What was that noise?" Walter asked Emily from the other room.

"It sounded like Buddy slamming into the wall and falling behind the couch," Emily guessed, completely accurately.

"There's no way we're leaving him alone here," said Walter. "He'll trash the place."

"You should take him to work with you," said Emily. "I'll bet he'll be very helpful."

Walter could not think of a worse idea, and he said as much, but Emily wouldn't budge.

 Chapter Eight

The next day, Buddy wore a brand-new suit to work. It went great with his elf hat. He followed a reluctant Walter to the Empire State Building.

"Hello, Walter," said a coworker once they were inside the elevator.

"Hi, Jack," Walter said.

"Hello, Jack!" Buddy yelled very enthusiastically.

Everyone stared at him, wondering who could be so happy when it was so early in the morning.

Stepping off the elevator, Walter said, "Hi, Sarah," under his breath.

Buddy waved. "Hi, Sarah. I love that purple dress. It's so purple!"

"How's it going, Walter?" asked another coworker.

"Hi, Francisco."

"Francisco!" Buddy shouted. "That's fun to say. Francisco!"

"Could you at least get rid of the hat?" Walter whispered.

"I like the hat," said Buddy. "I could try, but I really like it."

As soon as Walter sat down at his desk, Deb came in with a cup of coffee for him.

"Thanks, Deb," said Walter.

"Good morning, Deb!" said Buddy happily. "You have a very pretty face. You should be on a Christmas card."

"Uh, thanks, Buddy." Deb backed away from him carefully.

Walter wanted Buddy to read some books, but Buddy wasn't interested. "Francisco!" he sang, tossing the books to the ground. "Francisco! Francisco! Francisco!"

"We're cutting down on your sugar intake," Walter grumbled.

"Why is your name on the door?"

Walter smirked at him. "I bought the door. My name's there so no one steals it."

"Is that a joke, Dad?" asked Buddy.

"Yes." Walter nodded.

"This is your office, isn't it?" Buddy teased.

"Well, how do you like that?" Walter leaned back in his chair. "He's understanding sarcasm."

Buddy clapped his hands together and looked around. "So what are we going to build?" He was confused, because even though they were at work, he didn't see any tools.

"This really isn't that kind of office."

When the phone rang, Buddy beat Walter to it. "Buddy the Elf! What's your favorite color?"

"Please don't touch anything in here." Walter hung up the phone. Suddenly he had an idea. "Have you ever seen a mailroom before?"

"A mailroom?" asked Buddy excitedly. "No."

"Mail comes from all over the world to get sorted in one place," Walter told him.

"Wow!" Buddy said happily.

Walter rode with Buddy down to the basement, but then he left to return to his office. Buddy approached the mailroom door, hearing a lot of shouting going on.

"Welcome to the pit," the floor manager said as he showed Buddy around. Unfriendly men glared at him. "Over here is the trench. All the mail comes out of that shooter. You scan and find the floor each piece is moving to. Put it in a canister and shove it up the tube with the same number. Got it?"

"Yeah!" said Buddy. "I like tubes and canisters and numbers. This place reminds me of Santa's workshop. Except it smells like mushrooms and everyone wants to hurt me."

Buddy got to work, and within minutes he had mastered the process of sorting mail. He whizzed across the floor speedily. No one had ever seen anything like it, and they were all very impressed.

As he worked, Buddy began to sing. "*On the first day of Christmas, my true love gave to me, a partridge in a pear tree.*"

Ignoring the dirty looks from the other guys in the mailroom, he kept on singing. His voice was off-key and horrible, but for some reason, the song was infectious. Pretty soon, the entire room broke out into song.

"*Nine ladies dancing*," sang one man as he dropped a package into the chute.

"*Eight maids a-milking*," sang a bald guy in a spiked collar.

"*Seven swans a-swimming*," sang a tattooed man with a gruff voice.

"*Six geese a-laying*."

Everyone sang the chorus: "*Five Golden Rings!*"

Suddenly Walter walked into the room. The mailroom guys stopped singing. All but Buddy, that is. "*On the twelfth day of Christmas, my true love gave to me…*"

When he finally noticed his dad, his voice trailed off, and he smiled.

Walter did not.

Chapter Nine

On Thursday night, Buddy walked to Jovie's house and pressed the button next to her name. It buzzed loudly, which made Buddy jump back.

Five minutes later, Jovie came downstairs, asking, "Why didn't you come up?"

"I got scared," said Buddy. "You look miraculous."

"Miraculous? That's a new one. Thanks." When Jovie noticed Buddy still standing there, she asked, "So what do you feel like doing?"

"I have a few ideas."

"Well, I'm up for anything," said Jovie.

"Really?" Buddy said.

"Sure."

Buddy blindfolded Jovie and took her to a coffee shop. "Don't look. Just reach out and take a sip," he said.

"What are you doing?" Jovie took a sip and made a face.

"Well?" asked Buddy.

"It tastes like a bad cup of coffee," she said.

Buddy took off the blindfold. "Ha, ha. That's right—it's the World's Best Cup of Coffee!"

Next he took Jovie to a revolving door. "Isn't this great?" he asked as he spun around and around.

When he was finished spinning, Jovie took Buddy to the gigantic Christmas tree in Rockefeller Center.

Buddy marveled at the sparkling lights. "Amazing."

Next they went ice-skating.

Buddy was starting to like New York City.

Michael Gingsburg / © 2003 New Line Productions.

Chapter Ten

The next night was Christmas Eve. Buddy was walking around when he saw a familiar sight. Something blazed through the night sky, and it looked just like Santa.

It was Santa! He'd lost control of his sled, and seconds later he went diving down into Central Park.

Buddy ran to the scene frantically. When he arrived, he breathed a sigh of relief. The reindeer were grazing in the grass, and Santa was okay, too. He was trying to fix the sled, which had billows of smoke rising up from its engine.

"Santa!" yelled Buddy.

Startled, Santa jumped away and shouted, "Back off, slick!" But once he recognized Buddy, he gave him a hug.

"Are you okay?" asked Buddy.

Santa shook his head. "Boy, am I glad to see

Alan Markfield / © 2003 New Line Productions.

you. The Claus-o-Meter suddenly dropped down to zero."

"Oh no!" said Buddy. The Claus-o-Meter measured the amount of Christmas Spirit in the world. It was very important. Without a full tank, the sled didn't work, and if the sled didn't work, Santa couldn't fly. If Santa couldn't fly, there was no way for him to give away presents. Children all over the world would be disappointed. "This is horrible," said Buddy.

Santa nodded his head gravely. "There's almost no Christmas Spirit left in the world. I need an elf's help."

Buddy looked down and kicked at the grass. "But I'm not an elf, Santa."

"Buddy, you're more of an elf than anyone I've ever met!"

"Really?" said Buddy.

"Really," Santa replied. "Will you help me fix this thing?"

Buddy couldn't believe that Santa Claus— the real Santa Claus—was actually asking for his help! "Of course!"

Santa told Buddy that he'd lost some important parts of the engine before his crash, so Buddy ran into the woods to find them.

Soon after Buddy left, Michael and Walter walked by.

They saw a man in a Santa suit and some reindeer and the sleigh, but they didn't quite believe it was the real Santa Claus.

Alan Markfield / © 2003 New Line Productions.

So Santa decided to prove it to them. "Tell me, Michael," he said, "what did you want for Christmas?"

"I wanted a skateboard," said Michael.

Santa pulled out his list, flipped to Michael's page, and read, "Not just any skateboard. You want a real Huf board with high 145 Thunder trucks, and 52 millimeter Spitfire classic wheels, and some Swiss bearings."

Michael's eyes widened, and his jaw dropped. That was exactly what he wanted! He wondered if maybe there really was a Santa Claus.

Just then the Claus-o-Meter moved up, and the sleigh started to shake. It rose off the ground and wavered for a few seconds before crashing back down.

"What happened?" asked Michael.

"You made the sled fly," Santa explained. "It runs on Christmas Spirit. You believed in me, so you made the sled fly."

"Then fly away," said Michael.

"I'm afraid I need more than the Spirit of just one person to reach the sky."

Buddy came running back with the missing pieces from the engine. Once he put them back, the sleigh started to rise again. It shot off, but only slowly. Then it petered out and fell to the ground once more. Buddy continued to tinker with the motor.

"We need more Christmas Spirit," cried Santa.

A crowd had gathered in Central Park to see what was going on, and Jovie was among the spectators.

She thought about what Buddy had said

about singing in public. Maybe he was right, she realized. There was nothing wrong with Christmas Spirit, after all. She sang, *"You better watch out. You better not cry, you better not pout, I'm telling you why…"*

When everyone heard Jovie's beautiful voice, they decided to join in.

As more people sang, Santa's sleigh became more powerful. He and Buddy jumped in. Santa steered the reindeer, and Buddy continued to tinker with the engine. The sleigh was moving, but only very slowly. Santa and Buddy flew through the air unsteadily.

Michael looked at his father and noticed something strange. "You're not singing!" he yelled.

"Yes, I am," said Walter.

"No," said Michael. "You're just moving your lips!"

Walter tried to argue, but gave up. Then he belted out, *"Santa Claus is coming to town!"*

The Claus-o-Meter shot all the way up, and the sleigh soared high into the air.

Everyone kept singing as Santa's sleigh flew across the sky!

Thanks to Buddy, Christmas was saved!